Put Beginning Readers on the Right Track with ALL ABOARD READING™

The All Aboard Reading series is especially designed for beginning readers. Written by noted authors and illustrated in full color, these are books that children really want to read—books to excite their imagination, expand their interests, make them laugh, and support their feelings. With fiction and nonfiction stories that are high interest and curriculum-related, All Aboard Reading books offer something for every young reader. And with four different reading levels, the All Aboard Reading series lets you choose which books are most appropriate for your children and their growing abilities.

Picture Readers
Picture Readers have super-simple texts, with many nouns appearing as rebus pictures. At the end of each book are 24 flash cards—on one side is a rebus picture; on the other side is the written-out word.

Station Stop 1
Station Stop 1 books are best for children who have just begun to read. Simple words and big type make these early reading experiences more comfortable. Picture clues help children to figure out the words on the page. Lots of repetition throughout the text helps children to predict the next word or phrase—an essential step in developing word recognition.

Station Stop 2
Station Stop 2 books are written specifically for children who are reading with help. Short sentences make it easier for early readers to understand what they are reading. Simple plots and simple dialogue help children with reading comprehension.

Station Stop 3
Station Stop 3 books are perfect for children who are reading alone. With longer text and harder words, these books appeal to children who have mastered basic reading skills. More complex stories captivate children who are ready for more challenging books.

In addition to All Aboard Reading books, look for All Aboard Math Readers™ (fiction stories that teach math concepts children are learning in school); All Aboard Science Readers™ (nonfiction books that explore the most fascinating science topics in age-appropriate language); and All Aboard Poetry Readers™ (funny, rhyming poems for readers of all levels).

All Aboard for happy reading!

TO

Bianca & Madeline

A dog who thinks she's a cat,

and a cat who puts up with her.—M C-L

 Published by Grosset & Dunlap, a division of Penguin Young Readers Group, 345 Hudson Street, New York, New York 10014. GROSSET & DUNLAP and ALL ABOARD READING are trademarks of Penguin Group (USA) Inc. Printed in the U.S.A.

ISBN 0-448-43369-9 10 9 8 7 6 5 4 3 2 1

ALL ABOARD READING™

with 24 Flash Cards!

PICTURE READER

Calling ALL Cats

By Maryann Cocca-Leffler

Grosset & Dunlap • New York

I am having a birthday

party for my .

I set out 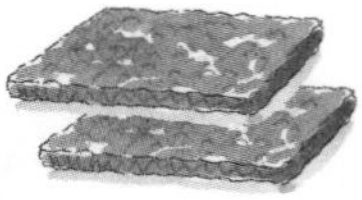 and .

I hang  and .

I make a .

It looks like a .

HAPPY BIRTHDAY MADDIE
MILK

I  down the street.

"Calling all  !"

I say.

"Come to my 

for a party."

"I do not have a ,"

Krissy says.

I watch her .

Her  plays

with a toy  .

Her  likes  .

Her  lies in the  .

"Your  thinks

she is a  !" I say.

"She can come

to the party."

There are 6 

at the party.

And 1  who thinks

she is a  !

I give them party  .

The party starts.

The 

and the 

play with the .

They drink 

in the .

It is time for the 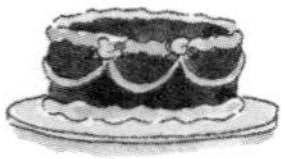 .

We sing "Happy

Birthday."

The 

and the 

eat the 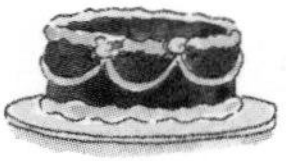 .

Then the  sleep

on the 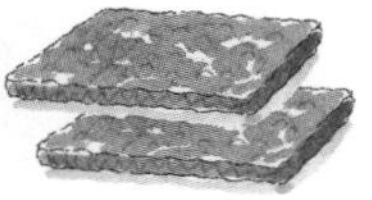.

But the  is not sleepy.

The  runs

to the 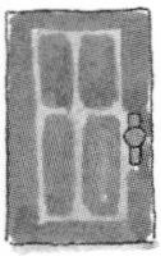.

She wants to play.

Ruff Ruff

The  gets the .

 do not do that.

The  jumps

through the 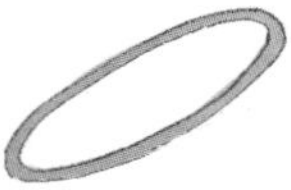.

 do not do that.

The  plays

in the .

 do not do that.

"Your  is

a !" I say.

The  goes

back in the 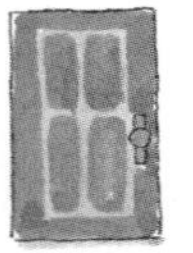.

Now the  finds

a .

The  sleeps

in the  . . .

. . . just like a  !

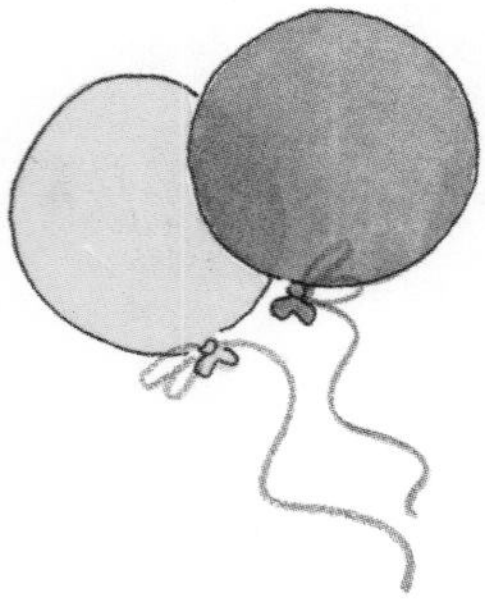

cat

balloons

mat

cats

yarn

bowls

fish

table

house

cake

sun

dog

6

1

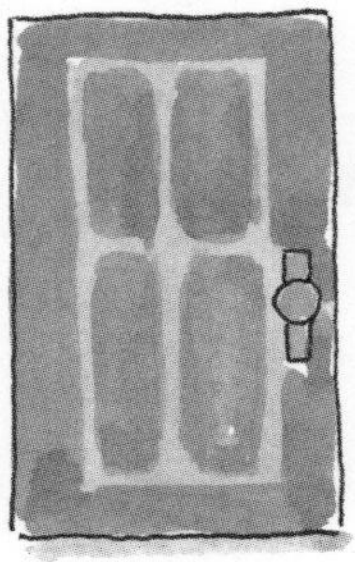

one	six
door	milk
water	ball

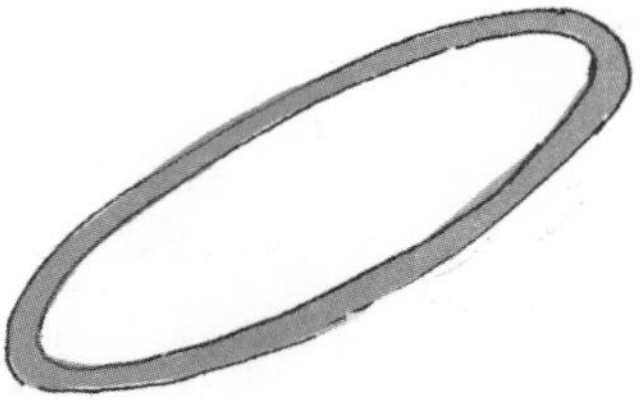

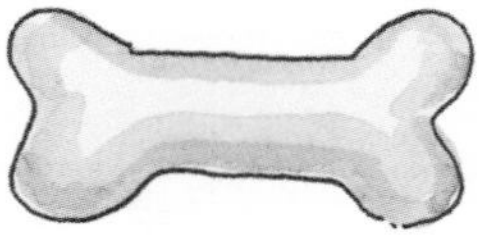

hats

hoop

mouse

run

window

bone